Also by Janet S. Wong
with pictures by Geneviève Côté

Minn and Jake's Almost Terrible Summer

Minn and Jake

Minn
and
Jake

Janet S. Wong

pictures by
Geneviève Côté

SQUARE
FISH

Farrar Straus Giroux
New York

SQUARE
FISH

An Imprint of Macmillan
175 Fifth Avenue
New York, NY 10010
mackids.com

Our books may be purchased in bulk for promotional, educational,
or business use. Please contact your local bookseller or the Macmillan Corporate
and Premium Sales Department at (800) 221-7945 ext. 5442 or
by e-mail at MacmillanSpecialMarkets@macmillan.com.

Library of Congress Cataloging-in-Publication Data
Wong, Janet S.
    Minn and Jake / Janet S. Wong.
      p. cm.
    Summary: Fifth-grader Minn, the tallest girl in school, begins a rocky friendship
with Jake, a new student who is not only very short, but is also afraid of the worms
and lizards that Minn likes to collect.
    ISBN 978-0-37440-021-7 (paperback)   ISBN 978-1-466-89484-6 (ebook)
    [1. Friendship—Fiction. 2. Individuality—Fiction. 3. Self-confidence—Fiction.
4. Teasing—Fiction. 5. Schools—Fiction.] I. Title.

PZ7.W842115 Mi 2003
[Fic]—dc21

                                        2002035421

Originally published in the United States by Farrar Straus Giroux
First Square Fish Edition: 2015
Square Fish logo designed by Filomena Tuosto

20 19 18 17 16 15 14 13 12

AR: 2.0 / LEXILE: 740L

To Jenny
my very tall true best friend from fifth grade
who taught me how to catch lizards
without breaking their tails

Minn and Jake

1 / Extra Lizardy and Alone

Do you ever feel
like

somehow

when you were out digging tunnels
or rescuing worms,
chasing lizards
or throwing rocks,
baking muffins
or sleeping—
somehow
when you didn't even know
it was happening—

you lost your true best friend?

And now you have no one
you can be your dumb self with,
no one
you can be your scared self with,
no one
you can be your selfish self with?

Do you ever feel this way?

This is the way Minn feels today.

Minn is feeling very empty,
and very tall,
and very odd,
and very pigtailed,
and very lizardy,
and very much alone.

Maybe
Minn feels empty because
all she had for breakfast
was a bruised banana,
eaten in ninety seconds flat
after she tied her shoes
in the car.

Maybe
Minn feels tall because
the class picture came back yesterday,
and she is standing a full head taller
than anyone else in her row,
the tall back row.
And the top of her head
is missing.

Maybe
Minn feels odd because
while they were standing
outside the classroom
waiting
for Mrs. Moss to unlock the door

before school,
Lola looked
at Minn's new red high-top sneakers
and whispered loud
to Sabina,
Is it Valentine's Day already
or were those shoes 50 percent off?

And Sabina,
Minn's true best friend
until last week,
covered her mouth
and whispered something
in Lola's ear,
and Lola busted up laughing.

And maybe
Minn feels pigtailed
and lizardy
and alone
because
Minn *is* pigtailed
and lizardy
and an only child,
the only only child in her class.

Whatever it is,
this morning
Minn is feeling

extra lizardy and alone,

and is wishing
she had a new true best friend,
someone
who would choose her
and keep her
for a true best friend, too.

2 / How NOT to Choose a True Best Friend

There are lots of good ways
to choose a friend.

You can choose a friend
because you like the same games,
or because you live on the same street,
or because your parents work together,
or because you need to borrow a pen.

Or you can choose a friend
because she smiles at you

and makes you feel good.

Minn is not smiling at Jake.
No one is smiling at Jake,
and Jake does not feel good.

His new teacher, Mrs. Moss,
is almost smiling.

She seems to be trying to smile,
but she has a worried look,
a look that says,
Boy, do I have a headache—
and how

are we ever going to finish this chapter
before recess?

And all the kids
are staring at Jake
wondering,

Who is this new kid?

Why is he coming into fifth grade
in the middle of the year,
in the middle of the week,
in the middle of Morning Reading?

How can a fifth grader
be so short?
He should be a fourth grader,
or a third grader,
or a second grader,
or a first grader,
or a kindergartner, even!

Everyone is staring at Jake

and Jake is staring back,
wishing
his father never took this new job,
wishing
his family never moved

away from Los Angeles
here to Santa Brunella,

wishing
he could move back today

to be with his old friends,
who never stared at him.

—

Jake knows
everyone is staring at him
because he is so short,
and maybe also
because he has a new spiky haircut
that he never asked for
that makes him look
like a baby crow.

Jake is feeling bad,
so bad
that he is starting to do
what he always does
when he needs to feel better,
which is
to turn everyone into animals.

That boy there
with the striped shirt

was a tiger in another life—

no, a snake.

This boy here
with the busy hands
and twitchy nose

was a housefly

who died
stuck between a shut window
and a screen
full of fried-chicken grease.

And her,
with the freckles
and the long legs
and the very long pigtails,

once upon a time
she was one giant

squid.

Jake is ready to turn his teacher,
Mrs. Moss,
into a

walrus—

then she says,
Pick a book off the shelf, Jake.
One of the blue ones.
Quickly!

Mrs. Moss is pointing
to the five-shelf bookcase.

Jake walks to the bookcase
and reaches for a book

off the bottom shelf.

No, Jake,
not one of those dark blue ones.
One of these light blue ones,
this kind.
They're mixed in with the others,
there,
on the number-four shelf, see?

Jake can see them all right,
there on the fourth-highest shelf,
two feet above his head.
He doesn't even bother reaching up,
because then everyone will see

that he cannot reach them.

This kind? he asks Mrs. Moss,
pointing to a turquoise-colored book
on the fourth-lowest shelf.

Oh no, Jake, no—
pick someone to help you get one, OK?
Go ahead, choose a friend to help you.
Quickly!

Jake looks around the room
at all the eyes.

There, in the corner,
glaring at him,
is Minn (the squid)—
the tallest kid
at Santa Brunella Elementary.

She is the tallest girl he has ever seen.
She is taller than Jake's mom.

When Minn is sitting
she is almost as tall as Jake is
when he is standing.

I'll bet she's tall enough to reach
the ceiling,
Jake is thinking,
looking at her long, thin fingers.

Her, Jake says, pointing to Minn.
The one with the red shoes.

Mrs. Moss says,
Minn, please stand up and get a—

RRRRRRRINNNNNNNG!

As Minn grabs a book for Jake,
everyone rushes out the door to recess,

leaving Minn and Jake alone
with Mrs. Moss, who says,
Stick together at recess, you two, OK?

3 / Stuck

The worst thing that can happen
in fifth grade

is being stuck all recess long
with someone you don't like.

But worse than that
is when you are stuck
all recess long
with someone you don't like

who doesn't like you, either.

Jake chose Minn, yes,
but he didn't choose her
to be his friend.
He chose her to pick a book
off the shelf.

Minn hates sticking out.
And she knows
Jake chose her because she stuck out,
because she is tall,

because of these dumb red shoes
her mother made her buy
because they were 50 percent off.

(She doesn't know that Jake chose her
because she is tall
and also
because he wonders
what the life of a reincarnated giant squid is like.)

Jake is practical, and a real diplomat.

Seeing as they're stuck together,
Jake is thinking
at least he and Minn should try
to be nice to one another.

So Jake says,
Thank you for helping me get the book.
What's your name, again? Minn?
What do you do for recess at this school?

Minn doesn't answer.
She is walking fast,
straight toward the field.

Four square?
Football?
Soccer?
Snacks?

Minn doesn't answer.
After they pass Miss Julie,
the recess teacher,
Minn breaks into a run.

Minn is running out to the field,

running twice as fast as any other kid,
shouting,
Come on!
Hurry up, Jake—
or it will be too late!

　　　—

Jake is not sure he wants to hurry.

But everyone is running to the field,
at least all the fifth graders,
so whatever is going on,
it must be good.
Hurry up! The worms!

Jake thinks, *Worms?*
At recess they play with worms?
But everyone is running,
so Jake starts to run to the field, too.

　　　—

Minn is almost there.
She turns around

to look back at Jake,
who is the slowest runner she has ever seen.

He is so slow
and so small
that he seems to be a quarter mile away.

Will he ever get here?

She is standing watching him
with her hands on her hips,
when screams
come out of the crowd
on the field.

Yuck! Oooooooh!
Don't! It's so disgusting!

Minn cannot wait any longer.
She turns and starts to run again.

The whole thing will be over

by the time Jake catches up.
Minn sprints to the field.
Three steps before she gets there,

screams come from the crowd again.

I don't believe he did it!
Wahooooo!
Yuck! Ugggh!
I told you!
Disgusting!

And then Henry bolts out of the crowd
and vomits in the bushes,

and wipes his mouth on his shirt,

and smiles.

Sabina screams,
Minn, you missed it!
Henry ate your worms!

But wait—
Vik's going to do it now—

RRRRRRRINNNNNNNG!

The rest of the day is no picnic.

Of course
Miss Julie tells Mrs. Moss
what happened
with the worms
and Henry
and the vomit,

and Mrs. Moss decides
that for one month
fifth graders are not allowed
on the field.

And for the rest of the year

there is to be
no more eating live creatures
of any sort,
bugs
or spiders
or worms
or anything

anywhere on school grounds.
No more playing with them,
either.

This last part really hurts Minn,
who loves more than anything
to watch the worms
wriggle across the mud.

When it is hot and dry,
too hot and dry for the worms,
Minn is the one who squirts the dirt
with the water bottle
she fills up at the drinking fountain.

—

This is how
she learned the rivers and lakes
of the United States
for the fourth-grade geography unit.

Squirt! Squirt!
The Snake River!

Squirt! Squirt! Squirt! Squirt!
The Mississippi River!

Squirt! Dig! Splot!
Crater Lake!

—

Minn takes care of her worms.

Once a week
she scoops up topsoil
in her two hands
from under the plum tree
near the school fence,
dark black soil
with bits of rotted plums mixed in,

and dumps it in the spot
where she knows the worms are.

Whenever it rains, after the rain,
Minn spends her recess time
searching the basketball court
for her worms.
When she finds them struggling,
she moves them back to the mud.

These were Minn's worms
that Henry ate.

Vik had dared Henry to do it
to show everyone that he (Henry)
is not in love
with Minn.

(And now everyone knows that he—Henry—
definitely *is* in love with Minn.)

—

This day
is turning into Minn's most rotten day.
Can it possibly get worse?

Yes,
it can get worse.
And it does.

Because

this is the day that Minn's mother
calls the school office
to say she is stuck in traffic

a very long ways
behind some kind of
must-be-an-accident
on the jam-packed
hate-this-stupid-bridge

and helicopters are flying around
and Minn's father is busy
in a meeting in the city

and so
yak yak yak
she will be an hour late,
at least.

Can you send Minn home with a friend?
Minn's mother asks.

Just leave a note on the classroom door
so I'll know where she is, OK?

But by the time the office tells Mrs. Moss,

all of Minn's friends
have been picked up
by parents who came on time.

All of the kids are gone

except for Jake

and his preschooler brother
and his mother who is busy
asking questions about homework.

The secretary has to leave now
for her dentist appointment,

and Mrs. Moss has to leave now
to pick her daughter up from school,

and the principal went home
ten minutes ago—

so Mrs. Moss asks,
Jake, you like to play with worms?

Before Jake can open his mouth,
Jake's preschooler brother screams,
Yes!

Jake's little brother is named Jefferson,
but almost no one knows his name.
Everybody calls him
Soup.

Soup as in, *What a super swimmer!*
And also soup as in,
What is this water in your bath—
it looks like mud soup!

Jake's little brother has been swimming
ever since he was six months old.

Soup loves water.

He swims like a fish.
He acts like a fish, even.
(When Jake is feeling bad,
he imagines that in another life,
Soup was krill,
which is a very shrimpy
kind of shrimp,
swallowed by the thousands
by penguins and whales.

Thinking of Soup as krill
always makes Jake feel much better.)

Soup is so much like a fish

that when he hears the word *worms*
his eyes get big and round and wet.

He gets excited,

so excited
he pees in his pants.

And then he takes them off, his pants—
and his underpants—
outside the classroom,
right in front of Minn.

Minn sits next to Soup
on the way home,

relieved that he is buckled
in his car seat,
with Jake's backpack on his lap.

When they get to Jake's house,
Jake runs in his room to hide.

Soup runs in his room

and runs back out again
with fancy cowboy pants on,
and fancy cowboy boots,
pointy-toed ones with real metal spurs.

I am Super Cowboy! Soup shouts.
And you are Minn the Horse!

Minn says,
I don't play horse.

Soup says, *Let me show you!*
He chases her into the corner
with his twirling lasso
and tugs on her hand.

Minn will not play horse.

So Soup starts to cry,
which makes Jake's mother stop
her onion-chopping
and shout from the kitchen,
Is everything all right in there?

Soup tugs on Minn's arm
again
and opens his mouth
in a fake cry

which looks real enough
to make Minn surrender.

Minn crouches
on her hands and knees.

Soup shouts,
Yes, everything's all right, Mommy!

And then he backs up
and runs forward
and jumps onto Minn's back
like a rodeo cowboy
so Minn
can send him
bump-bump-bump up high,

and side to side

like a cowboy
on a bucking bronco,
bump-bump-bump-buckaroo—
his feet flying,
his spurs spinning—

Oh no
oh no
oh no no no no no no no—CRACK! CRASH!

HELP!

31

The aquarium
full of fancy tropical fish

does not break
because of Soup's real metal spurs, no.

It is the kick of Soup's boot,
instead,
that shakes the old aquarium stand

just enough

to make it wobble,
wobble and fall in slow motion,
with the huge lava rock inside
falling, too—

Oh no
oh no
oh no no no no no no!—CRACK! CRASH!

And water is rushing out
the top of the aquarium,
sending fish tumbling
to the floor,
thirteen poor fish

who flip and flop

from one side to the other

on the fuzzy carpet

—

until Jake runs out of his room
and grabs his favorites,
Angelghost and Flick,
and runs with them to the toilet,

and runs back
and grabs Disposal and Plungerface,
and runs with them to the toilet,

and runs back
and grabs Ick and Uck,
and throws them into the toilet, too,

while
Jake's mother is trying to sponge up
the water from the carpet
with a handful of towels,

and Minn and Soup are trying
to grab
the slick
slippery
little blue ones—

which are so hard to grab
without squishing—

Yuck, squish, *sorry!*—

—

Soup!

I am so sorry, Minn's mother says.
I insist. Really.
Let us pay you back for this.
What a mess!
Minn never should have played
such a stupid game.

At least the fish are all right.
Plungerface, Disposal,
Ick and Uck,
Angelghost, Flick,
and the $2.99 Blue Kind
all are swimming
(scared, but swimming)
in the toilet,
except for the one
that got squished flat
by Soup.

Jake spent a whole week
coming up with names
that fit the fish—

Plungerface: the yellow one with the big nose
who likes to suck the side of the tank.

Disposal: the garbage fish,
the miniature catfish
who eats the old food and scum
at the bottom.

Ick and Uck:
the ones who always seem to have poop
trailing out their backsides.

Angelghost:
the silvery black-and-white angelfish,
so flat and skinny
there's hardly enough room
for real live guts
in her.

Flick: the black one
who likes to flick
her long flowing fins
into the other fishes' faces.

The last seven (six, now),
the little blue ones,
have easy names:
all of them
are called
the $2.99 Blue Kind,
which makes them feel like a team.

Jake got his fish just a week ago,
to replace the old fish he gave up
in Los Angeles
when they moved.

But they did not buy a new aquarium
or aquarium stand.
This tank that broke
was their old one from Los Angeles,
Jake's mother's tank
from when she was six years old,
set on her old metal stand.

So
since the fish are all right (mostly),
Jake is kind of happy
that the aquarium cracked,
since now he can get a new one.

But he doesn't want to let anyone see
how he really feels.
He wants Minn to think he is mad.
He wants Minn to suffer,
to feel awful inside.

And Minn's mother wants to make things right.
Please, please, please—I insist—
we want to do something to pay you back.
We'll do something fun.
I know:

Come to our house tomorrow after school, Jake.
That will be fun, won't it, Minn?

Minn has her arms crossed
and is staring out the living room window.

Jake's mother looks at Jake,
who has his arms crossed
and is staring out the living room window, too,
his back turned to Minn.

Minn's mother smiles at Jake's mother,
who says,
I'll pick him up at five tomorrow, OK?

Today is the next day
and Minn's mother is stuck in a meeting,

but today
Minn's father is working at home.
Minn says,
This means we're walking.

Walking? Jake says.
Jake hates to walk.
Why won't your father pick us up from school?

I like walking home.
It's fun—you'll see.
Mom doesn't trust me to walk by myself,
but Dad doesn't mind,
just as long as I'm home by four o'clock.
Minn is six feet ahead of Jake.
Two of her steps equal five of his.
Come on, get walking!
We have one hour to get there—
or my dad will be worried.
Hurry!

Minn and Jake are walking
one long mile

up the steepest hill in Santa Brunella
all the way to Minn's house.

And when you're walking a mile
up the steepest hill in Santa Brunella,
you stop whenever you can.

Their first stop
is the water tower in the woods.
Let's build water tunnels, Minn says.
There's a leak over on this side.

Jake plops down to rest.
He is exhausted.
While Minn builds water tunnels,
Jake takes a nap on the grass.

Their second stop is on the fire trail.

Here's a soap plant.
See these leaves?
When you find one,
pull the bulb up.
Dig your fingernails into it
and wash your hands.

I'm thirsty, Jake says.

There's a stream
in the Gulch,

back that way and over and down,
but don't go there, Jake.
You could break your bones
if you fall down the ravine.
Besides, if you drink that water,
the bacteria will bloat your belly
and you will die.

I'm really thirsty, Jake says.

The thing about a soap plant, Jake,
is you don't need water to wash.
Just rub the soap juice all over your hands
and spit—

While Minn digs for soap plants,
Jake takes a nap
in the shade of the oak tree,
dreaming that he is swimming
in a huge glass of cold lemonade.

—

Their third stop is the Screep.
Minn's great-grandmother is the one
who first called it that,
and now everyone calls it that, too.

A scree is a tumble-jumble of small rocks,
and the Screep is the scree
where everyone scrapes their knees up.

to Minn's house
the Gulch!
Water tank
c screep
p plants
up the hill
school

The Screep is Minn's favorite place in the world,
the place beyond the fire trail
where hundreds of prehistoric rocks
run down a brown grass slope
like a leftover avalanche.

The Screep is Minn's favorite place
because this is where Minn hunts—

and Minn lives for the hunt.

When Minn goes hunting,
it's not for eating,
or killing,
as you probably figured out.

Minn hunts for lizards,
which she likes to keep
for ten minutes or so
in the old peanut butter jar
she carries in her backpack.
The lid has holes poked in it for air.
She likes to watch the lizards
watch her.

Usually Minn can catch three lizards
in five minutes,
so lizard-hunting never takes very long.

But today
Minn has not caught a single one
in fifteen minutes.

It is 3:55, and they need to be home by 4:00 p.m.
And so
for the first time

Minn is really bothered
that Jake doesn't want to do
anything she tells him to do.

Minn is really bothered
that all Jake wants to do is loll around
on his back
and nap.

—

And so
she is not going to tell him
that right now
at this very moment,
as he is sleeping on the Big Arrow Rock,

a humongous lizard is starting to crawl
in the shadow of his face

and now it has one foot on his ear

and another on his cheek—
And no, Jake, don't swat, it's not a fly—

and its left foot on his nose
and—

AAAAAAAAAAAARGHHHHHHHHHHH!

—

Jake is awake now
and shaking his head like a wild dog
and spitting, spitting, spitting everywhere—

but all Minn can say is,

How'd you let that lizard get away?

All you had to do was open your mouth
and he would've fallen straight in—

what a waste of a really good lizard!

Jake was born
smack in the middle
of the city of Los Angeles,
the part of town
where mainly
there are apartment buildings
and houses
and offices and stores
and neat little patches of grass
the pest man comes to spray—

and no lizards.

—

So Jake's first thought on waking
with a lizard foot on his lips
was not what a waste of a lizard
but
instead was

AAAAAAAARRRRGGGH!

—

But Minn was born
in Santa Brunella,
where for miles and miles around
all there is

is open space
and rocks and tall grass
and lizards—

and her mother
and her grandmother
and her great-grandmother
and everyone born in Santa Brunella
grows up catching lizards
after school.

—

So Minn is mad
that Jake has wasted
such a good chance,
and she decides it is time
to teach him
a lesson.

Enough napping, Jake:
we will stay here until you learn
how to catch a lizard!

Stand toward the sun,
so your shadow—

But Jake's watch beeps,

which it does every hour on the hour,
from the time Jake sets the beeper
at seven o'clock in the morning

until the time Jake turns the beeper off
at nine o'clock at night.

—

And when it beeps,

Minn jumps, panicked, scared—
as if she were the one
who almost swallowed a lizard
in her sleep.

Oh, no! Four o'clock! Minn shouts,
stuffing her empty peanut butter jar
and notebook and pen
in her backpack.

Hurry up, Jake!
We've got to get home!
Dad will be worried—
and when he's worried, he gets really mad!
I might not get to walk home anymore!
Run!

Minn's father
is only slightly worried,
since he figures
Minn must be lizard-catching
with her new friend Jake.

Or teaching him how to catch lizards.

—

Minn's father did not grow up
in Santa Brunella
but he understands
how important
lizard-catching is
to kids who grow up here.

Minn's father grew up
smack in the middle of New York City
where he never saw a lizard,
but he did a fair amount
of critter-catching
as a boy—
cockroach-catching.

And he loves it, still.
Minn's father is so good
at catching cockroaches,
he can do it with a pair of barbecue tongs.

So he can understand
how Minn loses track of time
when she is at the Screep.
He is not at all worried.

—

Minn stumbles in the door,
covered with sweat,
her face streaked with dirt.

Minn is alone.

Now Minn's father is starting to worry,
and starting to get mad at Minn:
Where is your friend Jake?
Did you run and just leave him behind?
Is that the way to treat a friend?

Minn looks behind her.
Where is Jake?

She runs out to the street
and shouts, *Ja-A-ke!*
No answer.
Where is he?

—

Minn is now worried—and mad, too.
Is he lost?
Did he run the wrong way?

Did he tumble into the Gulch
and break his legs?

She and her father run toward the Screep
calling *Ja-AAA-ke!*

All of a sudden they see a car
turn the corner
and drive toward them—

Jake's mother.

He called me on his cell phone.
He keeps a cell phone in his backpack.
I know it's silly, but he says
you never know.
Anyway—
something about lizard feet, rocks,
running, falling, something—

He was talking a mile a minute.
He told me to come get him now.
He was frantic.
Where is he?

Jake's mother dials his number
on her cell phone.
No answer.

She hangs up,
gets out of the car.
Soup is starting to cry.
Jake is lost!

Jake's mother is biting her nails.
She is on her middle finger
when the phone rings.
It's Jake! his mother says.
Jake, slow down!
Hold on! What? Who?
Where is This Creep?

Minn is not going to waste her time

on that hopeless city boy Jake,
who is the slowest runner
and the laziest napper
and a good-for-nothing lizard-catcher, no.

She is not going to waste her time
becoming his friend,

because what on earth
could she do
with a friend like him?

—

But for the sake of tradition—
and after all it is a tradition in Santa Brunella
to catch lizards after school—

and especially
because he is such a puny thing
and is going to be teased something awful
for being short
(and she knows how bad it feels to be teased,
especially for something
you can't do anything about,
like your height),

Minn will take one day—today—

to teach Jake to catch a lizard.

—

It is Saturday morning
and the sun is shining
but the air is cold,
which makes the lizards want
to sit longer in the sun.

This is the perfect kind of day
for lizard-catching.

So Minn calls Jake up on the phone,
and in one very long breath says,
Hello Jake this is Minn speaking
would you like
me to finish your
lizard-catching lesson
now
on this very most perfect
lizard-catching day?

And Soup says,
Minn, the Bucking Bronco!
No, I can't play. Sorry!
I'm swimming today.
Bye!

And Soup hangs up.

This time
when Minn calls,
she asks
to speak with Jake.

When Jake gets on the phone,
Minn makes her offer.

She is smiling while she is talking, even,
because she cannot believe
what a good person
she is being right now.

And Minn wants to be good to Jake
because not only will Jake get teased
for being so short,
he will also get teased something awful
for being afraid of lizards,

which everyone is talking about
because Minn made a big mistake
and told Sabina yesterday
about Jake's lizard-lips adventure

and Sabina told Henry
who told Vik
who told Lola
who told half the fifth grade.

So anyway,
Minn says to Jake on the phone,
Why don't you come over today
for a lizard-catching lesson?

No thank you, Minn.
See you Monday.

Wait. Are you busy?

No.

You're sick. Are you sick?

No.

Then why can't you come over, Jake?
Won't your mother let you come over?

She probably would.

So?
Are you going swimming with Soup?

No.

Let's catch lizards, then!
It's a perfect day—

I don't want to, Jake says.
See you Monday.

And Jake hangs up.

It is not for nothing
that Minn earned the nickname Mad Minn
in first grade,

which became Mighty Mad Minn
in second grade,

which became Minn the Maniac
in third grade,

which became the Minnster last year.

Minn is mad,
mighty mad,
maniacally mad,
monstrously mad at Jake.

And she is also mad at herself
for telling Sabina
that Jake is afraid of lizards.

So Minn will not give up.
She will fix Jake's reputation as a coward
and teach him how to catch a lizard
whether he wants to learn
or not.

Minn asks her mother to call Jake's mother
and ask if he can come over to play.

Jake's mother asks,
Will there be any other kids there?
I mean, any other boys?
It would be nice
if there are some other boys there,
you know?

Minn's mother does not know.
But she says,
That is a very good idea.
So as soon as I hang up,
I will call to invite Henry and Vik.
Jake will like Henry and Vik!

Minn has three students arriving
for the Lizard Lesson
in half an hour.

Because even though Henry and Vik
and every fifth grader in Santa Brunella
know how to catch a lizard,
no one can do it like Minn.

—

Minn is rehearsing her speech
in the mirror:

Stand facing the sun,
so your shadow will stay behind you.

Don't run up to the lizard.
Creep low and slow.
Don't talk.
Hold your breath.

The breath part is really important,
especially for you, Vik,
because red licorice is not a normal smell
in the wild.

Pretend you are a tree.
Your hand is a branch
reaching over,
being blown by the wind.

Now—
seize the belly
and don't let go
when you feel the squirming
inside your hand.

That's how you catch a lizard.

—

Vik and Henry arrive at Minn's house together
five minutes early.

Vik has a handful of lilacs with him.
Minn sneezes. Achooo!
Vik laughs. He loves to make Minn sneeze.

Henry has an armful of empty peanut butter jars.
Henry dumps them into Minn's arms and says,
My mother washed them out for you.

Minn stuffs them in her backpack.

—

Jake comes to Minn's house ten minutes late.
By this time, Minn and Vik and Henry
are shooting baskets in the driveway.

Jake's mother says out loud,
loud enough for everyone to hear,
Look, Jake!
You had nothing to be afraid of—
they're not catching lizards, see?

Vik and Henry bust up laughing.
Jake scowls.

—

Minn leads the way to the Screep,
with Vik and Henry right behind her.
Jake is a long ways back.

When they get to the Screep,
Minn gives her speech,
with one little change:

The breath part is really important,
especially for you, Vik,
because chocolate caramel
is not a normal smell
in the wild.

—

Minn catches three lizards in five minutes,
as usual.

Henry says he has caught ten of them.
He doesn't like to keep lizards, though,

so there's no way of telling

if he has just caught the same one
and let it go
and caught it again
ten different times—
or really caught ten.

Henry says
that he has caught ten,
but the chance that each of his lizards
would have a limpy left foot
is very small.

Vik has caught two.
They are both very fat lizards,
and slow ones.

One of them
might be the same one
who put his foot
on Jake's lips the other day.

Vik is proud of his lizards.

It is not easy for Vik to catch lizards.
He is not very good at holding his breath.
Besides,
even when he does hold his breath,
the chocolate-caramel smell
seems to sneak out his nose.

Everyone is finished with lizard-catching
for today,
everyone is packed up and ready to go—

except Jake.

Jake has not caught a single lizard.
He is still trying, though,
which surprises Minn.

But whenever Jake tries to grab one,
he misses—

and after ten or fifteen misses
his knuckles are scraped up
so badly
from hitting the rocks
that they are bloody
and raw.

If Jake doesn't miss,
he catches just the lizard tail—

which then falls off in his hand.

Jake has six lizard tails behind him,
a lizard-tail trail scattered over the rocks.

Jake is standing still,
looking at the lizard-tail trail.

Vik says,
Somewhere, Jake,
six stubby lizards are watching you,
mad as boiled cucumbers.

Henry says,
Sure, a lizard can grow his tail back,
but it takes a very long while, in lizard time.
It would be as if
somebody pulled your hair out
and you had to run around
bald for a whole year—
Wouldn't that make you mad, too?
I think that would turn you into
a vicious, man-eating lizard!

Vik says,
They're going to follow you home, Jake.
They're going to crawl into your car
when your mom comes
and sneak into your bed at night,
and do lizard voodoo on you—

Minn tells them to shut up,
but not in time.

Jake is looking

at the trail of lizard tails
scattered behind him,
and he is feeling
all those lizard eyes on him,

and he is feeling
scared.

17 / Jake Makes a Deal

Jake knows
that he may not be very brave,
or very fast,
or any good at catching lizards,
and this makes him feel crummy.

But he doesn't feel too crummy,
because he knows that there is one thing
he is very good at:

making money.

—

And so
on this boring Sunday morning,
Jake decides
that he is going to do something fun:
make some money.

Jake is only ten years old,
but he has already made over $523,
which he keeps hidden
in a pair of dirty socks
stuffed in a smelly old pair of too small shoes
in the back left side of his closet
behind a plastic guard dog
named Sphinx
with glow-in-the-dark eyes.

Jake doesn't do the lemonade thing.
He doesn't sweep patios,
or pull weeds,
or deliver newspapers,
or baby-sit—
so how did he get so much money?

Jake sells.
Jake cleans up old used stuff—
his used stuff,
his mother's used stuff,
his neighbors' used stuff—

and he finds a way to sell it.
Jake knows how to make a deal.

Jake decides to call Minn.

And here's the deal, Minn.
I know you like to watch your lizards,
but they don't have room
to do anything interesting
in a peanut butter jar, really, do they?
So how would you like
to have my broken aquarium?

It's cracked, so we can't use it.
The whole piece of glass might break
if we put water in it.
Or the water will leak out.

But you could patch it up with a little bit of tape,
and turn it into a terrarium.

I'll let you have it,
if you want—

      —

Minn has never imagined having a terrarium.
Jake, would you really?

Sure, he says. *You could patch it up real nice.*
I'll let you have it
for—say—five dollars.
It cost us two hundred dollars
to buy a new one yesterday.
Soup says I should make you pay
more than five dollars,
since it was all your fault
that the aquarium broke,
but—

Silence. Breathing.

Well, what do you think?
Five dollars?

Minn says,
I don't think so, Jake,
and hangs up.

18 / Minn Makes a Deal

Jake knows
Minn wants to make the deal.

This is because
he is remembering
the way Minn looked yesterday

when she was watching her lizards
and writing down what they do.

Minn was watching the lizards
as if
they were interesting,
as if they were
the most interesting creatures
on earth.

Minn really loves watching lizards.

And those lizards do nothing
in their cramped little peanut butter jars.

An hour goes by.
Minn does not call.
Maybe she lost my phone number,
Jake thinks.

So Jake calls her up and asks,
Do you have my phone number?

I threw it away, Minn says.

*I thought you might not have it
anymore,* Jake says.
*I'll give it to you again, don't worry.
You know what I was thinking?
If you cover the crack in the side of the glass,
the lizards won't get cut.*

*You could cover it with duct tape on one side,
and a couple of postcards on the other side.
I have a cactus postcard from Arizona
and a pineapple postcard from Hawaii.*

Minn says, *Saguaro cactus,
the kind with the arms?*

*That's the kind! Wouldn't it be great?
When you bring lizards back from the Screep
and put them in the terrarium,
they'll think they're in Arizona! Or Hawaii!
What do you think, Minn?*

Silence. Breathing.

How much? Minn says.

How much do you have?

Two dollars.

How about three dollars,
and I'll give you the postcards for free.

Silence.

Are you still there, Minn?

Breathing.

What do you think, Minn?

I think I'm thinking.

I'm thinking, too.
I'm thinking
I'm sorry I said it was your fault, Jake says.
It was Soup's fault.
Not yours.

Silence. Breathing.

That was my mother's aquarium.
She's had it since she was six.
Can you imagine that?

All right, Jake, three dollars,
with the postcards
and the lava rock.

Four dollars,
with the postcards,
the lava rock,
and you know what?
I have a dog named Sphinx, Jake says.
He has glow-in-the-dark eyes.
Lizards
can see glow-in-the-dark
in the day,
I heard it on TV.
Well, snakes can—I think—
so lizards probably can, too.
Yours, for four dollars.

Deal, Minn says.
We'll pick it up tomorrow
after school.

Delivery's free, Jake says.
We'll bring it now,
and I'll help you build it, OK?

Minn and Jake
clean the terrarium glass
with vinegar water,
and then they tape
Jake's cactus postcard and pineapple postcard
over the crack in the glass.

Then they go outside
to make a good mix
of dirt and sand and leaves,
tiny pea gravel and chunky rocks.

They put the rocky mix in the terrarium,
but not just flat.
They build hills and valleys
and mountains.

Minn uses sticks
to build half a cave
near the front
so the lizards will have somewhere
to hide,
but she can still
see the lizards hiding.

Between two mountains
they make a swamp with some water

and three small ferns
and five big rocks.

The plastic dog named Sphinx
makes an excellent island
in the middle of the swamp.

—

Now it's time to catch a lizard.

It takes just thirty seconds.
They run back home from the Screep
with the lizard inside a peanut butter jar,
and they set the open jar inside the terrarium.

—

Minn is ready to watch and write:

Sunday, February 9, 2:00 p.m.

Weather:
sunny
much warmer than yesterday
about 75 degrees

Description of lizard:
5 inches including tail
kind of skinny
more gray than brown

(I wonder if lizards turn grayer
when they get old?)

jerks her head around a lot

(Is she nervous
because she got caught?)

found her (him?) in the Screep,
on top of the Small Arrow Rock

she likes to sit on the dirt
in the Ferny Swamp

seems afraid of the cave
or maybe
she's just not curious about it

ate two mealworms

⟶

Jake doesn't mind lizard-watching now.
Now he thinks
it's kind of fun actually,
as long as he doesn't have to touch
the lizard.

He likes telling Minn what to write
and seeing her write his words down.

At the end of an hour
of lizard-watching
and note-taking,
Minn catches the lizard
and puts her (him?)
back into the peanut butter jar.

They take the lizard back
to the Screep
and set her (him?) free.

Sitting on the Big Arrow Rock,
Minn asks Jake,
You're not afraid—are you—
of the things Vik and Henry said?

What things?
Jake says, but the way he is picking nervously
at his shoes,
Minn knows he knows what things.

That revenge stuff, you know.
You're not afraid of those lizards
who lost their tails,
are you?

Because, if you're worried,
I know a way
to make sure nothing bad will happen
to you.

Jake says,
Do I have to touch any more lizards?

Minn says,
No, and if we do it right,
the lizards will never bother you.
We'd make an offering,
to please the Lizard Gods.

Are you willing to give it a try?

20 / The Lizard Gods

Jake feels dumb.
And he feels like someone is watching him.
Creepy.

Have you done this before, Minn?

Sure, many times.

Many times?

At least twice, as a human.

As a human?

Well, I know this might sound kind of strange,
but have you heard of reincarnation?
In another life, I was a lizard.
I'm sure of it.
Either a lizard or—

Minn, don't tell me—
a giant squid?

Incredible!
How'd you know?

Minn and Jake are at the Screep
searching the rocks

for the six lizard tails that fell off,
the six lizard tails that Jake pulled off
yesterday.

Minn finds one and picks it up.
The tail doesn't look quite the same.
It is not fat and straight anymore.
It looks a little dried up,
and curly.

Like a dead tail would,
I suppose.

—

Think of them as fingernails, or hair,
Minn says.
Those lizards will grow new tails.
You did them a favor, really.
These are nasty old tails,
don't you think?
Now they can grow nice sleek new ones.

Minn is holding a handful of tails.

Jake can't stand the idea
of touching them,
so if he sees one, he calls for Minn
to come and pick it up.

They are missing just one.

The last one probably fell in a crack
between the rocks,
Minn says.
Let's get started with what we have.

—

Minn makes a circle
with the five tails,
a circle with the fat part of the tail
pointing in,
and the pointy part of the tail
pointing out.

This is looking very voodoo to Jake,
and he does not like the looks of it
at all.

Next, Minn reaches
into her back pocket
and pulls out a plastic pillbox.
She opens it and dumps the contents
in the middle of the circle.

Mealworms for the Lizard Gods,
she says.

The Lizard Gods?
Jake asks.

Minn explains.
The Lizard Gods watch over all the lizards.
If you offend the gods,
you need to make an offering.
Mealworms are best.
If you don't have any mealworms handy,
dead mosquitoes work.
French fries.
Even dried boogers.
I think they like the salty taste.

Minn grabs Jake's right hand
and rubs mud on it.

Hey! Jake pulls his hand back.
Why did you do that?

We have to read your future.
The lines in your hand tell the future.
Give me your hand.

Minn grabs it.

Look, your wilderness line is very long.
See that?
It looks weak here, in the beginning,
but then there's a little split, see—
That was when you lived in Los Angeles,
and here is now, in Santa Brunella.
You have a lot of wilderness

in your future, Jake,
so you'd better make peace
with the Lizard Gods.

—

Minn starts to sing
a chanty nothing-kind-of-song.

You stand on that side
of the mealworm offering, Jake,
and I'll stand on this side.
Sing like this.
Not a real song,
but kind of a breathy song.
You pretend you're a hot lizard.
Stick your tongue out like this,
and put your arms back,
and now
make short grunty exhales like this—
do it, Jake!
This will take away all your bad luck!

—

Minn and Jake are singing
the Breathy Song
with their short lizard arms pulled in
and their mouths open
and their dry tongues out—

when all of a sudden
two heads

pop up
out of the rocks below—

two heads
watching.

21 / Jake's Lizard Dream

That night
in Jake's dream
two heads pop up
out of the rocks below—

lizard heads.

The lizards creep forward.
Lizards without tails.

Suddenly
Jake hears thunder,
sees lightning crack a cloud in half—
a cloud that looks like a lizard,
a giant smoky-gray lizard.
The Cloud Lizard is doing the Breathy Song!

Bow down before Chameleus,
King of the Lizard Gods!

And now
hundreds of tail-less lizards are rising up,
twisting upwards in the sky,
floating into the cloud—

where—*zap!*—
their tails are fastened back,
and they rocket down to the ground,

headfirst,
tails straight as arrows,
headed straight for
Jake's mouth—

AAAAAAAARRRRGGGH!

That night
in Minn's dream
two heads pop up
out of the rocks below—

boy heads.

Henry and Vik!
They are cackling,
The Lizard Gods!
Ha!
What a liar—
and Jake believes her!

They have seen the whole thing,
the circle of tails,
the mealworm offering,
the singing of Breathy Song!

Vik is holding
his arms in close to his sides,
doing the Breathy Song.

And Henry is laughing,
pointing at Minn,
and holding
the lost last lizard tail.

23 / Two Heads

Two heads pop up
out of the rocks—

one! two!—

two

sleek

smooth

grayish-brown—

what do you think?—

gophers.

Monday morning is Sharing Time,
or Show-and-Tell,
in Mrs. Moss's fifth-grade class.

Some teachers
think fifth graders are too old
for Sharing Time,
but this is Mrs. Moss's fifth graders'
favorite part of the week.

Each week has a theme.
Last week's theme
was Foods from Nature.

One Sunday
(two Sundays ago,
when Minn and Sabina were still best friends),
they worked the whole day
making acorn muffins.
They gathered acorns
under the oaks on the fire trail
and blanched them in boiling water
to take away the bitterness.
Then they roasted them in the oven
and peeled them
and mashed the nuts into a paste.
They mixed the paste with cornmeal
and egg
and oil

and honey
and a tablespoon of baking powder
and a pinch of salt—
their own recipe.

It tastes awful, Sabina said.

You don't eat it alone, Minn said.
We need beef jerky and dried berries.

We need chocolate chips, Sabina said.

—

When Minn wasn't looking,
Sabina put a whole bag of chocolate chips in,
which definitely gave the acorn muffins
an unusual taste.

Minn and Sabina won a gold star
for Most Unnatural Food from Nature.

—

This week's theme
is Animals of the Wild.
Sabina has a small plastic crate
with something furry in it.

A chinchilla is a wild animal? Vik says.

Sabina throws three grapes into the cage.
See? Wild animal!

—

Minn has hauled her terrarium to school.
There is a lizard inside.
This one is small and fast
and likes to run around
and hide in the cave.

Vik has a fat cocoon
in a jar stuffed with leaves.
He plucked it off a tree
last week
and he is predicting
it will turn into a moth
before the end of this week.
No one else thinks it will.

Henry has a two-inch fish
he caught with a plastic bag
in the stream
in the Gulch.
It is in a jar
full of dirty brown water.

And Jake has a box of dirt.
What a loser! Henry says
when he sees Jake's box.
A box of dirt!

But Jake doesn't feel like a loser.
Jake feels like a winner.
He doesn't care what Henry thinks.
He can't wait to surprise Minn.

Because inside this box,
buried in the dark black dirt,
are worms for Minn!

Henry says,
Hey, Jake, Foods from Nature
was last week—
but I dare you to eat one now.
Or are you afraid of worms,
like you're afraid of lizards?

I'm not afraid, Jake says, and reaches in.
He digs down at the bottom of the box
and fishes around a bit,
and winces,
then pulls a clear fat yellowish-brown worm
from the dirt.

And before anyone can even yell EEEUUUW
he pops the worm in his mouth
and holds it there a second
with his eyes bugging out.
Then he chews,
making a face like it tastes something awful,

chews
and swallows.

But doesn't run to vomit
in the bushes.

BURP!

Jake reaches in for one more.
This time
he hands the big fat slimy wriggling thing
to Henry, saying,
You're not afraid of worms,
are you, Henry?

Tomorrow is Valentine's Day.

Mrs. Moss has three valentine rules:

1. Give a valentine to everyone, or to no one.
2. Make your valentines, don't buy them.
3. Bittersweet dark-chocolate truffles for me!

—

Vik and Henry are rushing
to make a valentine for Jake this morning,
because they forgot about Rule Number One.

If they don't give a valentine to him,
they can't give out
the ones they've already made
for everybody else.

And that will have been
a lot of work for nothing.

But how can you give a valentine
to someone you don't like at all?

—

Jake's valentines have been ready
since Sunday night,
when he made them
with Soup and his parents.

His mother separated five dozen
Oreo cookies
and scraped the white filling off
with a butter knife.

Soup used a hammer
to pound the dark cookie halves
into a crumbly, dirtlike mess
on a cutting board
covered with wax paper.

Jake's father
mixed Soup's cookie dirt
with brownie dirt,
and scooped the lumpy brown stuff
into small plastic bags.

And Jake put gummy worms
into the bags,
saving the root beer ones
(which look clear and fat and yellowish-brown
and almost real)
in a bag for himself,

which he buried at the bottom
of his Show-and-Tell box
under some real dirt
and real worms,

the fattest, ugliest, slimiest worms
he could find.

NOT!
Of course
Jake does not love Minn.

He likes Minn,
as a friend,
but not as a girlfriend.
The idea
that one day
he will have a girlfriend
who will want to smash her slimy lips
on him
is fairly repulsive to Jake,
and so
(except for the candy)
Valentine's Day
is one of his least favorite holidays.

And today is Valentine's Day.
The most gossipy day of the year,
when regular old likes
look a lot like love
to mischievous searching eyes.

—

Lola whispers,
Jake loves Minn
to Vik,

who says,
Jake loves Minn, pass it on
to Henry,

who runs to Sabina and shouts,
Ja-A-ake loves Mi-I-inn!

And now everyone in the class
is looking at Jake and Minn.

He did help her make the terrarium,
after all.
And he gave her worms.

And he ate one
and didn't even vomit it up.
And everyone knows
that the only reason
for eating a worm
is to prove you don't love
someone you really do.

It must be love.

Minn sees Henry's evil smile
as he hands Jake a valentine,
and she rushes over to Jake's desk
to try to warn him.

She doesn't know what will be inside,
but she figures it might be worms.

She doesn't get to Jake's desk in time.

Jake opens the envelope.
He pulls out a piece of paper
and unfolds it

and—AAAAAAAARRRRGGGH!—

a dried-up lizard tail
falls on his hand.

Jake keeps screaming
for at least three long seconds
and flaps his arms all over,
and the lizard tail goes flying up in the air
across the room—

and lands on Mrs. Moss's desk.

But the note
inside the valentine
stays on Jake's desk,

a dirty note with torn edges that says,
Remember me?
I know where you live.

NOT!
Minn does not love Jake,
even if
she did make him
a huge chocolate heart
out of melted chocolate
poured in a heart shape
and frozen in the freezer overnight.

Everyone knows
that Minn is not a lovey girl

since she does not love Henry
who has had a crush on her since first grade
and eats a peanut butter sandwich
every day
so he can give her empty jars
for lizards.

And everyone knows
that Minn is not a lovey girl

since she does not love Vik
who has had a crush on her since Christmas,
and puts flowers on her desk
whenever he finds some good ones to pick
so he can make her sneeze.

Everyone knows
that Minn is not a lovey girl,

but Minn is starting to wonder
if maybe
this feeling
she is feeling inside
right now
is not just a sorry feeling,
but—could it be?—
is she getting lovey after all?

She knew it would happen sometime,
but why now?
She is feeling a strong urge
to put Jake in a headlock
and give him a noogie
on top of his spiky little head.
Why him?

Ja-A-ake loves Mi-IN-nn!
Henry says again.

Minn scowls,
glaring at her valentines—

and drops her bag of worms
on the floor.

February is the time
when the snow melts
in the mountains
one hundred miles north
of Santa Brunella,

so February, of course,
is the worst time
to climb down into the Gulch.

In August,
the stream in the Gulch
isn't strong enough
to wash a toothbrush,
but in February—watch out!

Minn's great-grandmother says
a boy got washed down to the ocean
in that February river once,
when she was ten years old.

He was eleven.

They had just finished giving out valentines
at school.
He gave her a red velvet heart,

pasted on a real piece of lace,
her one and only valentine from a boy.

She didn't give him one,
because he had only said hello to her twice.
How could she have known that he liked her?

For years she wished
she had made an extra valentine,
just in case.
She felt awful about it.
(There was no Mrs. Moss then,
and no Rule Number One.)

His name was Danroy,
and he was a good climber,
and a good swimmer,
an excellent lizard-catcher,
and he knew the Gulch.

But the boys who climbed down there
that Valentine's Day seventy-five years ago
got to throwing rocks,
and somehow
a rock hit the side of Danroy's head,
or maybe
hit him between the eyes,
and he went under.

They think he got caught under another rock,
downstream. Maybe.
They never found the body.

—

Today is the seventy-fifth anniversary
of Danroy's drowning.

Minn's great-grandmother
has been invited to speak at the school
to tell the story,
to honor the memory of Danroy,
and to keep the children of Santa Brunella safe.

Except
they don't all seem to want
to be safe.

Minn's great-grandmother
may be eighty-five years old,
but her hearing is as good as any lizard's—
and she can feel it,
she can feel the whispers in the room,
mischievous whispers
coming from some certain
troublemaking fifth graders
named Henry and Vik.

—

Because the only thing more exciting
to Henry and Vik
than climbing down into the Gulch

is climbing down into the Gulch
when you're not supposed to.

You have rocks in your head!
The river's too high!
Sabina knocks her knuckles against Henry's head.
You want to get drowned?

We did it last week, Henry says.
It was easy, like taking candy from a baby—

Or the tail off a lizard, Vik says.

Minn knocks her knuckles against Vik's head.
The weather's warming up.
That's what my great-grandmother is saying.
The water's getting stronger every day.
Now is not like last week, Vik.

But Lola whispers,
Henry, Vik! I dare you!

I dare you is Lola's favorite line.

Lola's dare made a certain girl whose name
starts with S and ends with A
dance down the street
stark naked
at midnight.

Lola's dare made a certain girl whose name
starts with M and ends with N
eat a can of dog food
at a slumber party
then kiss Lola's dog on the mouth.

And Lola's dare is exactly
the excuse that Henry and Vik were hoping for.

Henry and Vik
do not sneak down to the Gulch.

They march and yahoo to the Gulch,
and Lola tells all their friends to follow,
to watch

because
you can't prove how brave you are
unless people are there

to ooooooooh
and aaaaaaaaah

and see the veins pop out of your neck
when you slide down
the steep sides of the ravine,
your fingernails ripping
as you try to find something to grab on to,
a rock—*tumble!*—
a handful—*ouch!*—of thistle,
whatever you can grab
to keep from sliding fast down—*boom!*—
to the bottom

where the river is growing fuller
by the hour.

Don't vomit down there! Lola shouts,
and then Lola and Sabina giggle.

We're not going to eat any worms!
Vik shouts back.
Lola and Sabina giggle.
Minn scowls.

—

Who's going next? Lola asks.
I dare you, Jake.

Jake is too small to climb down there!
Sabina says.
Don't do it, Jake!
You'll get swallowed up!

Prove that you're not in love with Minn,
Lola says. *Go down in the Gulch!*

Minn is ready to push Lola
down into the Gulch
face first.
Don't be stupid, Jake!

Jake is not stupid.
There is no way on earth
he is going to go down into that gulch,
not now,
not ever,
never.

It makes Jake dizzy
just to watch
Vik and Henry
throwing rocks down there.

What about you, Minn?
Lola says.
Say it's true, you're in love with Jake—
or if you're not,
I dare you to go down into the Gulch
with Henry and Vik
to prove—

HELP!
H-E-L-P!
Vik is screaming.
Somebody! Henry went down!
Help! In the river! HELP!

Minn scrambles
down the steep side of the ravine.
No one can climb down into the Gulch
like she can.
She is holding on to a small tree,
a raggedy tree growing in the rocks.

It is bending low
and lower,
but not low enough for Minn to reach the next
ledge—
darn these silly slip-ons!
Her left shoe has just fallen off.

She should've worn her red sneakers.

Minn is fifty feet above the river,
ten feet down from the top of the ravine,
as high as on a roof,
and dangling,
hanging on the bent tree,
holding onto rock
with three fingers
and a good-for-nothing slip-on clog—
hanging off-balance,
ready to fall.

Vik is shouting,
Hang on, Minn!

Lola says,
Look, she painted her toenails!

Henry jumps out of the bushes,
shouting,
I'll rescue you!

Henry isn't in the river?

Sabina screams at Henry,
You stupid little joker!
Look what you did!
You stupidface, Henry!
Hang on, Minn!

Lola is laughing.
When did she paint her toenails?

Sabina turns to Lola and scowls.
Where is Jake?
Jake will have a good idea.
Jake is smart.
Where is Jake?
Ja-A-ake!
Is he really the coward everyone
thinks he is?

Jaa-AA-ke! Sabina shouts again.
Jaa-A-ke!

—

Two minutes later,
two minutes that feel like an hour
of yelling
and crying
and sweating
and the slow-motion bending
of the raggedy tree,
and Henry and Vik trying to climb up,
and rocks breaking off in little chunks
(since it's even harder to get out of the ravine
than it is to slide down into it),

two minutes later
a siren comes screaming—
a small fire truck
is here at the Gulch.

And Jake is running,
as fast as he has run in his whole life,
running with his backpack bouncing up
behind his head,
and his cell phone in his right hand,

and a plastic bag in his left hand,
a plastic bag
with half a huge almost-melted chocolate heart—

Jake is leading the way
for the rescuers!

Sabina is struggling
to give Jake a big hug,
and Jake is struggling
to get out of it.

Lola is trying to grab Jake's
cell phone,
and Jake is shoving it
in his pocket.

Jake is inching
over to the edge of the Gulch,

close enough so he can see Minn
climb up the rescuers' rope
(but not close enough to fall).

—

Minn's head rises up,
smiling.
When Minn reaches the top,
she rushes over to Jake

and gives him a big kiss
on the top of his head.
She and Sabina are hugging Jake
so tightly
that he is about to suffocate.

And everyone—
except for Lola,
who is starting to walk home—

is crowding around Jake,
patting his head,
or slapping his back,
or rubbing his shoulders,
or squeezing his hands,

and Jake feels his big heart
melting completely
to mush.

Happy Valentine's Day, Jake!

As you can imagine,
Minn is in big trouble.

But as you can also imagine,
Vik and Henry
are in even bigger trouble.
No one hugged Vik and Henry
when the rescuers brought them up.
No one told them how brave
and how smart they were.
Not even Lola,
who is telling everyone
that Vik and Henry should have known
she was joking,
that's how stupid they are.

Everyone saw that Vik and Henry
were safe
and then they left,
without saying anything.

And without saying anything,
they all knew

that this is the way it would be
for the rest of the school year,
for as long as Vik and Henry live in this town,
until they are ninety years old, even.

No one talked to them,
no one listened to them,
no one screamed when they threw spaghetti
in the lunchroom.
No one asked them,
Why are you wearing a caterpillar mustache?
or
What is that smell in your backpack?
Not even Mrs. Moss.

Vik and Henry
became invisible,
nobodies,
untouchables—

until
today,
the last day of school.

Jake and Minn
are on their way to Minn's house,
but first
they are going to catch lizards
in the Screep.

Minn has been grounded
for four whole months,

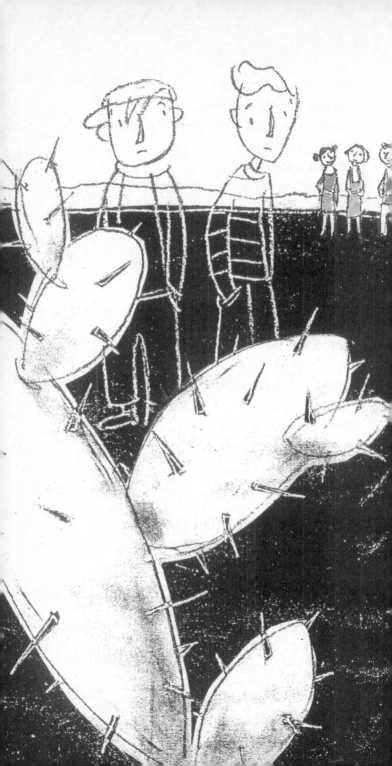

and this is her first day of freedom,
in celebration
of the end of the school year.

But what are Vik and Henry doing here?
Their parents have grounded them,
haven't they?

Caught a lizard yet, Jake? Vik shouts,
Or only tails? Henry asks,
and throws a rock at Jake's feet.
Four months of being untouchables
and Vik and Henry are even meaner than before.

Ignore them, Jake, Minn says.
But Jake doesn't want to ignore them.

Why are you guys so mean? Jake asks.

Why are you guys so mean? Henry repeats
in a sassy high voice.

Why didn't you ever say sorry?

Why didn't you ever say sorry? Henry repeats.
Why? You want to know why?
Because there was no reason to say sorry.
We made a funny joke—and you ruined it!
There wouldn't have been any trouble
if you hadn't called 9-1-1.

We would've helped Minn back up to the top.
No one got hurt. Nobody would've, either.
You turned our little joke into one great big mess.
Why didn't you ever say sorry to us?

Jake can't think of a thing to say.
This is the first time he has thought of it that way.
Everyone has been telling him he was a hero,
but maybe Henry is right.
Maybe no one would have been hurt.
If he hadn't called 9-1-1,
Minn wouldn't have been embarrassed
and grounded for four months.

You're a fink, is what you are, Henry says.

He is not! Minn says,
spitting mad.
But now that the evil thought has been said,
Minn can't help thinking, too:
maybe things would have been better
if Jake hadn't overreacted.
Why is Jake such a city boy?

City fink! Henry says,
as if he is reading Minn's mind.
I wish you'd go back where you came from!

Finkfinkfinkfinkfinkfink! Vik says,
crinkling his nose.

Finkfinkfinkfinkfinkfinkfink! Henry says,
and jumps up and down.

The sound of Henry and Vik's finking
sounds an awful lot like the Breathy Song.
All of a sudden
the clouds begin to rumble
and crack—

Run!

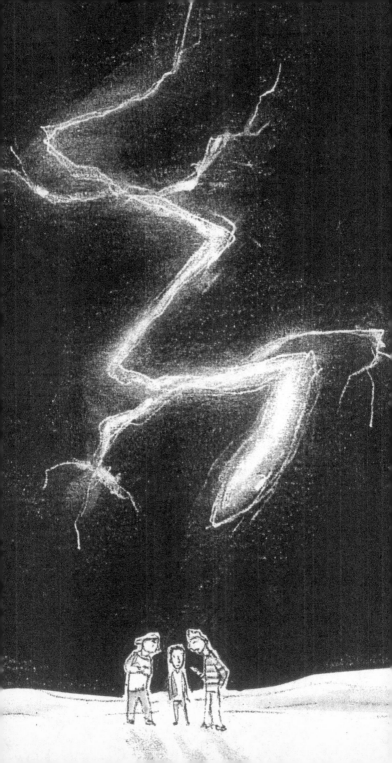

After the thunderstorm,
Jake tells Minn
the one thing
that will make Henry and Vik happier
than anything.

Jake is leaving Santa Brunella,
moving back to Los Angeles.

Why, Jake?
You don't want to move back, do you?

My grandmother is sick,
so my mother is taking us,
Soup and me, there to keep her company.
My father will stay here and work.
It's just for the summer.
We'll be back in September.

Minn cannot believe her rotten luck.
That empty odd pigtaily feeling
is starting to come back.

Stay here, with your father, Jake.
You can visit your grandmother half the month,
and come back half the month.
We could have a lot of fun in the summer.
I thought about your money-making idea,
and I'm ready to do it!

Minn's Terrariums!
We can make a terrarium a day,
and sell it for $20!
My mother says she can sell at least ten
at her office.
Just think, we'll be rich!

Jake is thinking of his old friends,
and how they used to collect stuff together,
and clean it up,
and sell it
at a table outside his house.

Jake misses his old friends.
He misses riding his bike on flat sidewalks,
and eating *churros* at the zoo,
and taking the bus to the beach.

But he will miss Minn, too.
Maybe she could visit,
and stay a few weeks.
Maybe she could stay half the month
in Santa Brunella
and half the month in Los Angeles?

Minn, you could visit us,
in Los Angeles.
My grandmother doesn't have a big apartment.
But there's room for you on the couch.
We could ride the bus
all the way down Wilshire Boulevard
to the beach,

and build tunnels in the sand.
Two blocks from my grandmother's house
there is a pet store
where they have bearded dragons
and green iguanas.
We won't need to catch our own lizards.
No more dull gray lizards—
we'll walk to the pet store every day
and watch iguanas and chameleons!

Minn is staring at Jake, shaking her head,
with her mouth open.
Minn is thinking,
How can it be
that my new true best friend Jake
doesn't understand that I like—love—
catching lizards?
Dull gray lizards?
Beautiful gray lizards!
How could he possibly think
that watching lizards in a pet store
could be as much fun?

And they have corn snakes
and parrots
and jellyfish—
Minn, it could be so much fun!

Silence. Breathing.

Minn feels cold.

And empty,
and tall,
and odd,
and pigtailed,
and very lizardy
and alone.

Minn is feeling very cold,
wet from the storm.
Call your mom.
You'd better go home, Jake.
You need to pack for Los Angeles.
See you in September.

Jake leaves,
and Minn takes a very long bath,
one of those
hold-your-breath-and-soak-your-head baths
that makes ideas float out your ears
to where you can see them more clearly.

A thought floats out Minn's left ear:

I have lost
my old true best friend, Sabina,
and now I am losing
my new true best friend, Jake.
What is wrong
with me?

And a thought floats out Minn's right ear:

Nothing is wrong
with you, silly.
Jake is still your true best friend.
He needs to visit

his sick grandmother.
Maybe you should try
to go to Los Angeles, after all!

Another thought floats out her left ear:

You've ruined everything.
Hope he forgets by September.

Another thought floats out her right ear:

Call him!

Not knowing the right thing to do,
Minn does the next best thing:
she goes to sleep.

She wraps her long wet hair in a towel,
and even though
it is only 4:30 in the afternoon,
she closes her door
and pulls her curtains shut
and makes her mind watery
and blank,
remembering her life
as a giant squid.

Minn sleeps so deeply
she sleeps through her mother shouting, *Mi-I-inn!*

She sleeps through her father shouting,
Dinnertime!
She is wandering
through the world of dreams:

Something is chasing me—
it wants to cut me in half
with scissors
but I am running,
running away—jump!

Now
I am some sort of an animal—a horse,
or a large cat.
What is that burning smell?

Here is Jake.
But small and bald and fat
like a baby.

I hand him a jar.
Here is a lizard I caught for you, Jake.

Eat her up, and you can grow big.

Jake shakes the lizard out of the jar
and holds her behind the head.
He lifts her up to his mouth
and he kisses her—

AAAAAAAARRRRGGGH!

Minn wakes up
with the soft mushy taste
of burnt marshmallow
in her mouth
and spit on the side of her face
and her pillow.

She sits still,
with her eyes shut,
trying to remember more of her dreams,
until she remembers,
Jake is leaving this morning!

Minn runs down the stairs.
Her father and mother
are reading the newspaper.
Minn knocks over her father's coffee.

Drive me to Jake's house—
What time is it?
Hurry! Please, please, please!

It is 6:15 a.m., Saturday,
and Jake and Soup and their mother
need to be at the airport in an hour.

Jake and Soup
and their mother and father
waddle out the door
with their suitcases.

Jake's father is packing
the suitcases in the trunk

just as Minn and her father
drive up, waving.

—

Minn knew! Soup says,
running into the house.
Minn came
because she knew!
I'm going to give it to her!

No, don't! Soup! Jake shouts.
Dad, stop him!

Give it to me? Minn says.

Something I got for you.
Last night.
My dad is going to take it to your house
later on,
after he drops us off
at the airport.

What is it? Minn wants to know.

Nothing. You'll get it later, OK?
Why'd you come? Jake wants to know.

I came to say goodbye, Jake.
And to ask if it really would be all right
to visit Los Angeles.
I mean, for me.
If my parents let me.
Do you really think it would be fun
if I came to visit—

A LIZARD!

Soup hands an empty honey jar
to Minn,
a honey jar full
of a lizard,
a lizard without a tail,
but with a note folded up
and placed inside:

Dear Minn,

I never thought
I would want to catch a lizard,
but you have taught me
to look at a lot of things
in a brand-new way.

I will miss you
this summer.

Your buddy,
Jake

Minn wipes the sweat from her hands
onto her pajama pants.
Where did you—
Did you catch this, Jake?

I caught him! Soup shouts.

We caught him, Jake says.
Well, you caught him,
but I taught you how—
I taught you exactly what Minn
taught me—
It was the most amazing thing, Minn—
it's almost like the lizard
was waiting

to be caught,
wanting to be caught,
just sitting here on the front steps—

—

Minn shakes the lizard out of the jar
and grabs him behind the head.
She lifts him up to her mouth
and she kisses him—

AAAAAAAARRRRGGGH! Jake shouts.

Oooooooooooooh, let me kiss him, too!
Soup begs,
but Minn drops the lizard
back in the jar
as Jake's father pushes the two boys
into the car.

Goodbye, Minn! Jake and Soup shout,
waving out the car window.

Call me on your cell phone!
Minn shouts back,
waving goodbye.

—

And up in the clouds,
the Lizard Gods are waving, too.